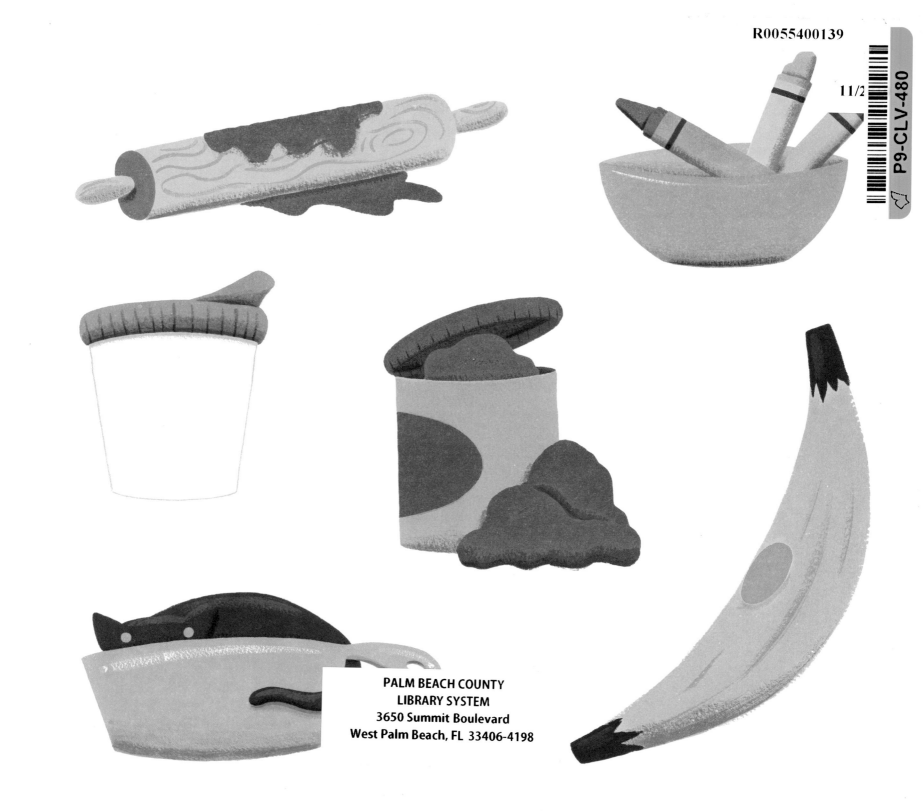

To my two little chefs.

— C. P.

Mine, too!

— D. Y.

A FEIWEL AND FRIENDS BOOK An Imprint of Macmillan

COOKING WITH HENRY AND ELLIEBELLY. Text copyright © 2010 by Carolyn Parkhurst. Illustrations copyright © 2010 by Dan Yaccarino. All rights reserved. Distributed in Canada by H.B. Fenn and Company, Ltd. Printed in June 2010 in China by South China Printing Co. Ltd., Dongguan City, Guangdong Province. For information, address Feiwel and Friends, 175 Fifth Avenue, New York, N.Y. 10010.

Library of Congress Cataloging-in-Publication Data Available

ISBN: 978-0-312-54848-3

Book design by Rich Deas
Feiwel and Friends logo designed by Filomena Tuosto

First Edition: 2010

10 9 8 7 6 5 4 3 2 1

www.feiwelandfriends.com

COOKING WITH
HENRY AND ELLIEBELLY

By Carolyn Parkhurst

Illustrated by Dan Yaccarino

Hello! I'm Henry, and this is my little sister, Eleanor, but I like to call her Elliebelly. Welcome to our show, *Cooking with Henry and Elliebelly*.

Cooking!

Today, we'll be making raspberry-marshmallow-peanut butter waffles with barbecued banana bacon. And now, here's our theme song:

Cooking with Henry and Elliebelly!
This show is good, this show is great.
We cook the food, but not the plate.
Cooking with Henry and Elliebelly!

Cooking! I help!

Now before we get started with our recipes, we need to put on our chef hats.
No chef hat. Pirate hat.

No, Elliebelly, this is a cooking show, remember? We *need* to wear chef hats.
NO CHEF HAT! PIRATE HAT!

Okay, you can wear your pirate hat, I guess.
Henny pirate hat! HENNY PIRATE HAT!

MOM!!!

What is it?

Elliebelly says I have to wear a pirate hat.

HENNY PIRATE HAT! HENNY PIRATE HAT!

Sweetie, she's two. You don't have to do what she says.

She won't stop saying it!

Work it out, you two.

Baby Anne!

Okay. Welcome back to *Pirate Cooking with Henry, Elliebelly, and Baby Anne.*

Cooking!

Now, for raspberry-marshmallow-peanut butter waffles, you need to get the finest ingredients possible.

We start with about seventeen cups of imported flour from Kansas, and mix it in a bowl with two jars of peanut butter and twelve duck eggs.

Pizza! I help! No! You can't put pizza in it! Pizza! Me do it!

Then mix everything together with a whisk made of the finest metal possible.

Baby Anne go swimming!

Mom!!!

BACk

Baby Anne take bath. That's right. Baby Anne is taking a bath in the washing machine. She'll be back later in our show. Getting back to our waffles, next you have to count how many years old you are: That's how many marshmallows and raspberries you need to add. So, my waffle will have five of each, and Elliebelly's will only have two.

Not two! Five! Five for Elliebelly! Sorry, Elliebelly. That's what the recipe says.

And now, it's time for a commercial. Buy a car! Buy a giraffe! Buy a rocket ship! Buy some pudding! NOW NOW NOW NOW NOW!!!

Nownownownownow!!!

Welcome back. Now, there are two ways you can make barbecued banana bacon: You can start with bacon and add bananas, or you can start with bananas and add bacon. It's really up to you. And while that's in the oven, let's check on our waffles. You want them to be crisp but not crunchy, brown but not black, hot but not cold.

I help cook. Actually, Elliebelly, our food is just about ready. Maybe you could help me eat it.

Eating! I help!

Mmm, delicious.

Where food, Henny? Well, it's just pretend food. We have to pretend to eat it.

No pretend food! Real food!

Try a bite. You can really taste the marshmallows.

Real waffles! I help eat!

Join us next time for *Pirate Cooking with Henry and Elliebelly*.

Baby Theresa!

And Baby Theresa. Bon appétit!